OPEN

The Small Mart is open! Time to go Shopkin searching with some of the super-cute characters who live here!

TACO TERRIE

This Tex Mex is full of beans and can go a bit over the top! Then he starts to become hard to handle! He loves dancing around sombreros with his bestie, Lammy Lamington.

SNEAKY SALLY

A real sneaky mover with a bouncy personality! This cheeky Shopkin loves being a step ahead of her friends when she's on the basketball courts.

COLLECT THEM ALL!

SUZIE SUNDAE

A Shopkin with a lot of glass! She's nuts about ice cream and can whip up a yummy treat in seconds! You can find her chilling out with her best friend, Kylie Cone.

CHATTER

Chatter loves to talk and is a very good listener. Her dream is to get married. All she wants is to be engaged and keeps looking for the perfect ring!

CASPER CAP

The Shopkin who can cap off any outfit and is always in peak condition! Loves playing baseball with his bestie, Flappy Cap.

CHEEKY CHOCOLATE

This Shopkin is definitely cheeky and a real prankster! She's always laughing and having fun and is never afraid to get dirty.

CHEE ZEE

A confident and passionate performer who loves taking center stage and is a little bit crackers! Find him rapping in the Dairy aisle with Cheezey B. and Freezy Peazy!

MOLLY MOPS

Molly Mops is buckets of fun! She's a real hard worker with a shiny personality. When it comes to finding a bargain, she loves to clean up!

DUM MEE MEE

Dum Mee Mee is a peacekeeper that was born to shop! She's no dummy when it comes to stopping tears and loves rocking out with babies!

JUICY ORANGE

Maybe a little bit pushy, but she's sweet on the inside. She's great at keeping juicy secrets. Find her in the Fruit and Veg aisle with her bestie, Sour Lemon.

TOASTY POP

A guy with a warm personality who never has a stale idea! He's always popping up with new stuff! Find him in Homewares throwing parties and giving toasts!

BEAUTY BONANZA

The Shopkins are hunting for some beautiful bargains. Can you spot all the Health and Beauty Shopkins hiding in the boutique?

LOOK FOR THE **LIMITED EDITION** SHOPKIN!

Ring-A-Rosie

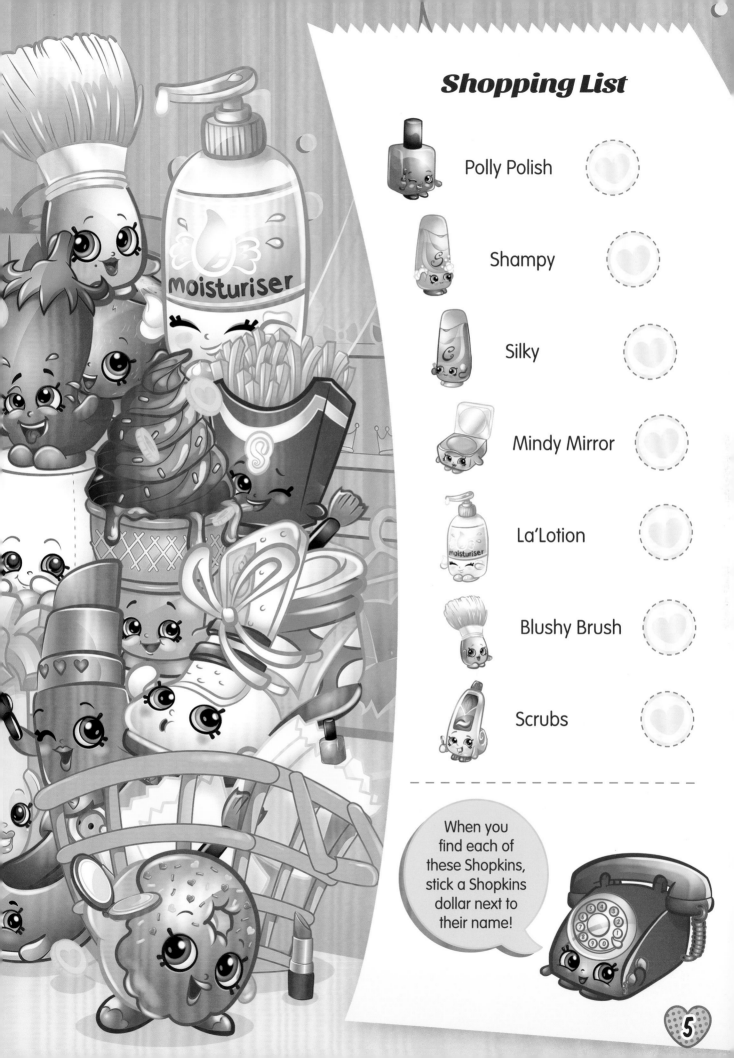

Shopping List

Polly Polish

Shampy

Silky

Mindy Mirror

La'Lotion

Blushy Brush

Scrubs

When you find each of these Shopkins, stick a Shopkins dollar next to their name!

SUPERMARKET SENSATION

The Shopkins are going wild in the aisles! How many of the Shopkins on Taco Terrie's list can you find?

Shopping List

 Cupcake Chic

 Kooky Cookie

 Peachy

 Pineapple Crush

 Cheeky Chocolate

Stick a Shopkins dollar sticker next to each Shopkin's name when you find them!

LOOK FOR THE
LIMITED
EDITION
SHOPKIN!
Brenda Brooch

BAKERY BLISS

The Bakery Shopkins are using Flour Power to cook up some tasty treats! Use your loaf and help Toasty Pop spot them all.

LOOK FOR THE
LIMITED EDITION
SHOPKIN!

Roxie Ring

Shopping List

- Toastie Bread
- Cheese Louise
- Patty Cake
- Fifi Fruit Tart
- Carrie Carrot Cake
- Slick Breadstick
- Pretz-elle

Pop a Shopkins dollar sticker next to each Shopkin's name when you find them!

9

BURGER JOINT

Chee Zee is looking for his bestie, Cheezey B. Can you spot all the other fast food Shopkins in the Shopville Burger Joint?

Shopping List

 Cheezey B

 Curly Fries

 Taco Terrie

 Rolly Roll

 Tommy Ketchup

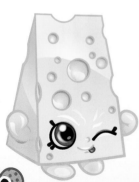

Don't forget to stick a Shopkins dollar next to each character's name when you find them!

10

LOOK FOR THE
LIMITED
EDITION
SHOPKIN!
Ticky Tock

HEAVENLY HOME

The Shopkins are in Homeware Heaven!
Can you help Chatter spot six differences
between these two busy pictures?

DISCO DISCOUNT

The Shopkins are feeling the groove at the Shopville Disco! Help Sneaky Sally find all the other disco divas hiding on the dance floor.

LOOK FOR THE **LIMITED EDITION** SHOPKIN!

Chelsea Charm

Shopping List

 Posh Pear

 Penny Purse

 Strawberry Kiss

 Candy Kisses

 Suzie Sundae

 Pumkinella

 Prommy

Don't forget to put a Shopkin's dollar sticker next to the other dancing divas when you find them.

FASHION SPREE

The Shopkins are always in fashion! Help Suzie Sundae find all of her stylish Fashion Friends.

Shopping List

 Heels

 Betty Boot

 Shady

 Kelly Jelly

 Casper Cap

Don't forget to stick a Shopkins dollar next to each character's name when you find them!

LOOK FOR THE LIMITED EDITION SHOPKIN!
Ruby Earring

17

ICE CREAM DREAM

The Frozen Shopkins love chilling out with their friends! Help Kylie Cone find six differences between the two pictures.

Frozen

SPENDING SPREE

The Small Mart is closing...It's the Shopkins last chance to grab a bargain! Help Cheeky Chocolate find the Shopkins on her shopping list.

LOOK FOR THE
LIMITED EDITION
SHOPKIN!

Donna Donut

Shopping List

- Fairy Crumbs ♡
- Wobbles ♡
- Wishes ♡
- Lolli Poppins ♡
- Le'Quorice ♡
- Jelly B ♡
- Bubbles ♡

Sweet! Stick a Shopkins dollar sticker by each Shopkin's name when you spot them.

Shopkins™
Once you shop...You can't stop!

EXTRA FUN

It's time to grab your bags and head back to the beginning! See if you can spot these extra Shopkins hiding on every page.

APPLE BLOSSOM

POPPY CORN

LIPPY STICK

D'LISH DONUT

PEE WEE KIWI

FIONA FRIES

ANSWERS

Check out your answers here.

Pages 4–5

Pages 6–7

Pages 8–9

23

Pages 10–11

Page 12-13

Pages 14–15

Pages 16–17

Page 18-19

Pages 20–21